# Canada

by Tracey Boraas

**Content Consultants:**
John D. Blackwell, Research Officer, and
Dr. Laurie C.C. Stanley-Blackwell,
Associate Professor of the Department of History,
St. Francis Xavier University, Antigonish, Nova Scotia;
Authors of "Canadian Studies: A Guide to the Sources"
http://www.iccs-ciec.ca/blackwell.html

# Bridgestone Books

an imprint of Capstone Press
Mankato, Minnesota

Bridgestone Books are published by Capstone Press
151 Good Counsel Drive, P.O. Box 669, Mankato, Minnesota 56002
http://www.capstone-press.com

*Library of Congress Cataloging-in-Publication Data*
Boraas, Tracey.
    Canada/by Tracey Boraas.
    p. cm.—(Countries and cultures)
    Includes bibliographical references and index.
    ISBN 0-7368-0766-7
    1. Canada—Juvenile literature. [1. Canada.] I. Title. II. Countries and
cultures (Mankato, Minn.)
F1008.2 .B67 2002
971—dc21                                                    00-009830

Summary: An introduction to the geography, history, economy, culture, and
people of Canada.

**Editorial Credits**
Gillia Olson and Connie R. Colwell, editors; Lois Wallentine, product
    planning editor; Sara Sinnard, cover designer; Heather Kindseth,
    interior designer; Kia Bielke, illustrator; Katy Kudela, photo researcher

**Photo Credits**
AP/Wide World Photos, 31; Archive Photos, 24; Canadian Identity Directorate,
57 (coat of arms); Canada Tourism Commission, 8, 14, 36, 41, 44; Capstone
Press/Gary Sundermeyer, 55; David Falconer, 4, 32; Digital Stock, 1 (center);
Hulton Getty Collection/Archive Photos, 27; Index Stock/Mick Roessler, 43;
Kennan Ward/Corbis, 19; Kit Kittle/Corbis, 46; North Wind Picture Archives,
22; One Mile Up, Inc., 57 (flag); Photodisc, Inc., cover (both), 1 (left, right),
20–21, 48, 56, 63; Stock Montage, Inc., 28; Thomas Kitchin/TOM STACK &
ASSOCIATES, 17; TRIP/W. Fraser, 52; Unicorn Stock Photos/Aneal Vohra, 34;
Unicorn Stock Photos/Jeff Greenberg, 50–51; Visuals Unlimited/
E. C. Williams, 10

**Artistic Effects**
Corbis; Capstone Press; Photodisc, Inc.

**Reading Consultant:**
Dr. Robert Miller, Professor of Special Education, Minnesota State University,
Mankato

1  2  3  4  5  6  07  06  05  04  03  02

# Contents

## Fast Facts about Canada

**Official name:** Dominion of Canada

**Location:** northernmost country in North America

**Bordering countries and waters:** United States, Pacific Ocean, Atlantic Ocean, Arctic Ocean

**National population:** 31,281,092

**Capital:** Ottawa

**Major cities and populations:** Toronto (4,263,757); Montreal (3,326,510); Vancouver (1,831,665); Ottawa/Hull (1,010,498); Edmonton (862,597)

# Chapter 1

# Explore Canada

Thousands of years ago, glaciers slowly moved across Canada. These giant ice sheets carved Canada's landscape. They created much of the country's magnificent scenery, including Banff National Park.

Banff National Park is located on the eastern slopes of the Rocky Mountains. The park covers 2,564 square miles (6,641 square kilometers) of mountains, forests, and wetlands. Glaciers continue to scrape the land in the northern area of the park. Banff also has three areas of natural hot springs.

Banff is one of Canada's most visited places. Visitors can explore Castleguard Caves, the longest cave system in Canada. Hoodoos attract many tourists. Wind and water formed these giant rocks into strange shapes. Campers and hikers often visit Banff. They can see Banff's variety of wildlife, including grizzly bears, bighorn sheep, mountain goats, deer, and woodland caribou.

◀ This swimming pool in Banff National Park holds water from the park's natural hot springs.

## From Sea to Sea

Canada's motto, "From Sea to Sea," describes the country's boundaries well. Canada is bordered on three sides by oceans. The Pacific Ocean washes against the western coast, and the Atlantic Ocean lies to the east. The Arctic Ocean makes up the country's northern border. The United States, Canada's only neighbor, lies to the south and west. Canada is divided into 10 provinces and three territories.

Canada's motto also hints at the country's size. Canada is second only to Russia in size, covering 3,851,788 square miles (9,976,141 square kilometers). Canada's population is relatively small for its size. About 31 million people live in Canada. In comparison, the United States has a population of 276 million and covers a slightly smaller area of 3,717,796 square miles (9,629,092 square kilometers).

About 70 percent of Canada's land is undeveloped. Much of this land is in the north. About 20 percent of the world's remaining wilderness areas lie in Canada. Even with huge regions of untouched land, Canada is one of the world's most advanced nations. Plentiful natural resources, modern industries, and new technologies have helped Canadians maintain one of the world's highest standards of living.

ARCTIC OCEAN

N
W E
S

Ellesmere
Island

Alaska
(United
States)

Kalaallit
Nunaat
(Greenland)

Inuvik

Victoria
Island

Baffin Island

Yukon
Territory

PACIFIC OCEAN

Whitehorse

Northwest
Territories

Territory of
Nunavut

ATLANTIC
OCEAN

British
Columbia

CANADA

Hudson Bay

Alberta

Saskatchewan

Manitoba

Newfoundland and Labrador

Vancouver
Island

Edmonton

BANFF
NATIONAL
PARK

Québec

Vancouver

Calgary

Ontario

New
Brunswick

Regina

Winnipeg

Prince Edward Island

Scale
Miles

0   150   300   450   600

0   200   400   600   800
Kilometers

UNITED
STATES

Montreal

Québec

Halifax

Nova Scotia

Ottawa

Toronto

## Geopolitical Map of Canada

**KEY**

⭐ Capital

● Cities

▨ National Park

〰 Trans-Canada Highway

## Fast Facts about Canada's Land

**Area:** 3,851,788 square miles (9,976,141 square kilometers)

**Latitude/longitude:** 60 degrees north latitude, 95 degrees west longitude at Canada's geographic center

**Highest elevation:** Mount Logan, 19,550 feet (5,959 meters)

**Lowest elevation:** Atlantic Ocean, sea level

**Provinces and territories:** Alberta, British Columbia, Manitoba, New Brunswick, Newfoundland and Labrador, Nova Scotia, Ontario, Prince Edward Island, Québec, Saskatchewan, Northwest Territories, Territory of Nunavut, Yukon Territory

# Chapter 2

# The Land, Climate, and Wildlife

Rugged mountains, thick forests, broad plains, and frozen tundra are some of Canada's many landscapes. Canada can be divided into seven land regions according to land features and climate.

## The Appalachian Region

Canada's Appalachian Region includes the eastern provinces of New Brunswick, Nova Scotia, and Prince Edward Island, as well as part of Newfoundland and Labrador. Much of the area contains hills and plateaus covered with farmland and forests. The hills and plateaus drop to rocky shorelines and sandy beaches along the Atlantic coast. The St. Lawrence River empties into the Atlantic Ocean. This shipping route to the Great Lakes brings many products to the interior of North America.

◀ The movement of Atlantic Ocean waters created these rock formations in the Bay of Fundy between New Brunswick and Nova Scotia. The tides here are the highest in the world.

The Atlantic Ocean's currents give the Appalachian Region a mild climate. Winters average 24 degrees Fahrenheit (minus 4 degrees Celsius) in the region's largest city, Halifax, Nova Scotia. Halifax's summer temperatures average 62 degrees Fahrenheit (17 degrees Celsius). Halifax receives an average of 56 inches (142 centimeters) of precipitation each year.

## The Canadian Shield

The Canadian Shield is Canada's largest land region. This rocky landmass circles Hudson Bay and includes the mainland of Newfoundland and Labrador, northern Québec, most of Ontario, northern Manitoba, northeastern Saskatchewan, and southern Nunavut. Hudson Bay's Lowland also lies in this region. It is one of the world's largest wetlands.

Bare rock, forests, and freshwater lakes cover the Shield region. Thousands of years ago, glaciers scraped away much of the soil. But forests of spruce, pine, and tamarack trees still grow in the thin layer of soil that remains. Thousands of lakes dot the area. The Laurentian Mountains lie in the eastern part of the region.

The climate in the Shield region varies from north to south. The north has long, cold winters and short summers. The climate of the south is more moderate, with warmer winters and summers. Low amounts of precipitation fall throughout the region.

## The Great Lakes-St. Lawrence Lowlands

The Great Lakes-St. Lawrence Lowlands region lies in southeastern Canada. The region includes the southern parts of Québec and Ontario. Three of the Great Lakes— Lake Erie, Lake Ontario, and Lake Huron—border the region to the west and south. The St. Lawrence Seaway

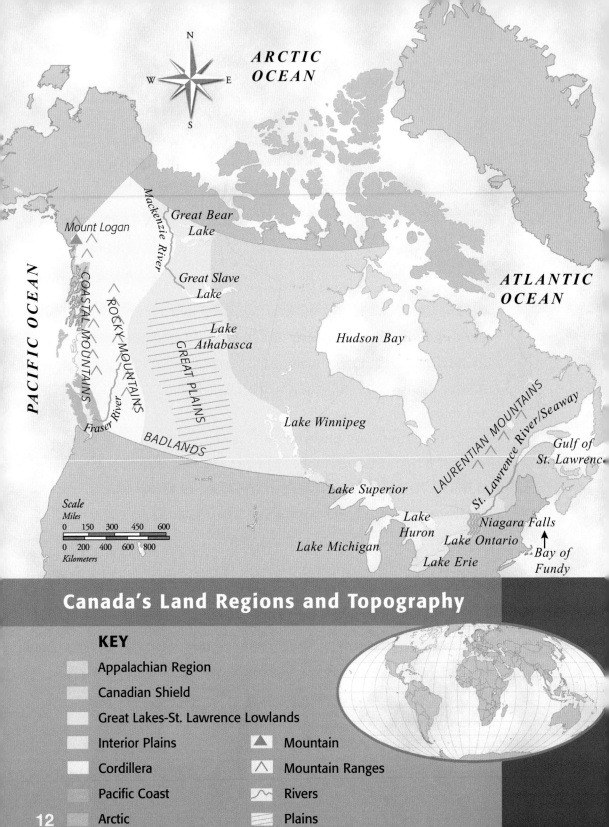

ARCTIC OCEAN

N
W   E
S

PACIFIC OCEAN

Mount Logan

Mackenzie River

Great Bear Lake

Great Slave Lake

COASTAL MOUNTAINS

ROCKY MOUNTAINS

GREAT PLAINS

Lake Athabasca

Fraser River

BADLANDS

Hudson Bay

ATLANTIC OCEAN

Lake Winnipeg

LAURENTIAN MOUNTAINS

St. Lawrence River/Seaway

Gulf of St. Lawrenc

Scale
Miles
0   150   300   450   600
0   200   400   600   800
Kilometers

Lake Superior

Lake Huron

Lake Michigan

Niagara Falls

Lake Ontario

Lake Erie

Bay of Fundy

# Canada's Land Regions and Topography

## KEY

- Appalachian Region
- Canadian Shield
- Great Lakes-St. Lawrence Lowlands
- Interior Plains
- Cordillera
- Pacific Coast
- Arctic

- ▲ Mountain
- ⋀ Mountain Ranges
- 〰 Rivers
- ╱ Plains

flows along part of the southern boundary. Niagara Falls lies on the border between Ontario and the U.S. state of New York.

The Great Lakes-St. Lawrence Lowlands region is called Canada's Heartland because of the rich farmland, many industries, and large number of people in the region. About 70 percent of Canada's manufactured goods are produced here. The region includes the capital city of Ottawa, as well as Montreal and Toronto, which are Canada's two largest cities. About 50 percent of Canada's population lives in the Lowlands Region.

Winds blowing off the Great Lakes keep temperatures mild in the region. Average temperatures in Toronto are 72 degrees Fahrenheit (22 degrees Celsius) in July and 23 degrees Fahrenheit (minus 5 degrees Celsius) in January.

## The Interior Plains

Flat grasslands and rolling hills stretch across the plains of Manitoba, western Saskatchewan, Alberta, and the southern Northwest Territories. This region is called the Interior Plains. The dry, desertlike Badlands lie in the province of Alberta. A cool, forested area known as the

▲ Green valleys lie between the mountains
of the Cordillera region.

parkland belt is located in the northern part of the region. The southeastern part of the region is called the Breadbasket of Canada. This area of the country is well known for its grain farming and cattle ranching. Edmonton and Calgary in Alberta, and Winnipeg in Manitoba, are the three largest cities in the region.

The Interior Plains region has cold winters and warm summers, with low levels of precipitation. The average January temperature for Saskatchewan's capital, Regina, is 2 degrees Fahrenheit (minus 17 degrees Celsius), while the average July temperature is 66 degrees Fahrenheit (19 degrees Celsius). This region of Canada averages 14 to 19 inches (36 to 48 centimeters) of precipitation per year.

## The Cordillera

The Cordillera is an area of mountains, high plateaus, and valleys in western Canada. Mountain ranges run south from the Yukon Territory through British Columbia. The Rocky Mountains, Coastal Mountains, and other ranges lie in this region. Mount Logan is the highest point in Canada. It rises 19,550 feet (5,959 meters) in the southwestern Yukon Territory.

Temperatures in the Cordillera vary from summer to winter. In the town of Whitehorse in the Yukon Territory, July temperatures average 57 degrees Fahrenheit (14 degrees Celsius). January temperatures average minus 2 degrees Fahrenheit (minus 19 degrees Celsius). Precipitation is light throughout the Cordillera.

## The Pacific Coast

The southwestern coast of Canada has the most moderate climate of all Canada's regions. The air from the Pacific Ocean keeps temperatures warmer in the winter and cooler in the summer. A temperate rain forest climate exists on the coast of British Columbia and on nearby Vancouver Island. These areas can receive more than 100 inches (254 centimeters) of precipitation per year. A thick forest of the oldest and tallest trees in Canada thrives in the wet climate.

Glaciers cut fjords into the Pacific region's coastline thousands of years ago. These narrow inlets make it difficult for ships to dock. An important flat inlet is the Fraser Valley. At the mouth of this river valley is Vancouver, one of Canada's major ports and the third largest city in the country.

## The Arctic

Canada's northernmost region, the Arctic, includes parts of the Northwest Territories and parts of the

▼ Huge moss-covered trees grow in the temperate rain forests on Canada's Pacific coast.

Territory of Nunavut. Inuvik, with about 3,300 people, is the largest community in the region. Canada's longest river, the Mackenzie, flows through the Northwest Territories.

A frozen desert called tundra covers the Arctic region. The ground under the topsoil is permafrost. It remains frozen year-round. In the summer, the topsoil thaws to a depth of 2 to 6 feet (.6 to 1.8 meters).

Winters are very cold and long in the Arctic. In Inuvik, temperatures average below freezing for 8 months out of the year. Average yearly temperatures in Inuvik are 16 degrees Fahrenheit (minus 9 degrees Celsius). The warmest month in Inuvik is July. Then, the average daily temperature rises to only 57 degrees Fahrenheit (14 degrees Celsius).

During the short summer, daylight is nearly continuous. Temperatures that sometimes climb as high as 86 degrees Fahrenheit (30 degrees Celsius) melt snow and ice. This water cannot drain or be absorbed into the ground because of the permafrost. The land becomes swampy and tiny wildflowers grow.

▼ This photo, taken from Lancaster Sound off Baffin Island in Nunavut, shows the harsh landscape of the Arctic.

## Wildlife

Canada's wildlife is as varied as the seven regions of the country. Different climates around the country create many habitats. The forests of British Columbia are home to cougars, bald eagles, and wolves. Grizzly bears thrive in the forests of the Yukon Territory and Northwest Territories.

Large and small animals live in the Arctic. Caribou and musk ox roam the tundra. Polar bears and white tundra wolves prey on these animals. Arctic foxes also make their homes here.

Many animals live in Canada's rivers, lakes, and oceans. Harbor seals dive in the Gulf of St. Lawrence. Walruses, dolphins, and killer whales swim in the northern part of Hudson Bay. The Arctic Ocean is home to narwhal whales and seals. Lakes provide homes for ducks and geese.

A variety of animals live on Canada's plains. Deer, coyotes, beavers, elks, and moose roam the prairies. Songbirds, such as wrens and meadowlarks, make their nests in the area. Rattlesnakes slither through the region's tall grasses.

# Polar Bears

Polar bears roam the Arctic tundra of northern Canada. They live on land, but they also swim in the water and walk on the ice.

Polar bears are known as fierce predators. They use their sense of smell, sharp claws, and strong jaws to catch and eat seals, their main source of food.

Polar bears have adapted to their environment in several ways. Polar bears are covered with long, clear fur. The fur appears white because it scatters and reflects light the same way snow does. This white appearance helps the bear blend into its surroundings.

A polar bear's skin helps it keep warm. The skin is black to soak up the warmth of the sun. Polar bears also have a thick layer of blubber beneath the skin, which keeps them insulated against the Arctic cold.

▲ Polar bears spend much of their time in Arctic waters.

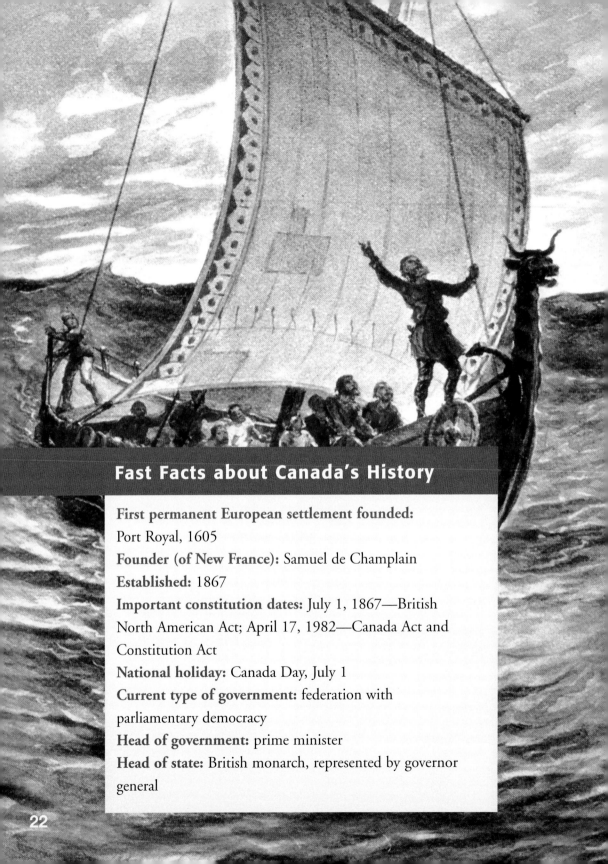

## Fast Facts about Canada's History

**First permanent European settlement founded:**
Port Royal, 1605

**Founder (of New France):** Samuel de Champlain

**Established:** 1867

**Important constitution dates:** July 1, 1867—British
North American Act; April 17, 1982—Canada Act and
Constitution Act

**National holiday:** Canada Day, July 1

**Current type of government:** federation with
parliamentary democracy

**Head of government:** prime minister

**Head of state:** British monarch, represented by governor
general

# Chapter 3

# History and Government

Some scientists believe that the first people to live in North America arrived 11,000 to 20,000 years ago. They may have traveled across a land bridge that once connected Russia and Alaska. Some of these early travelers settled in Canada. Today, the modern relatives of these original settlers are called Aboriginal Peoples or First Peoples.

## European Exploration

Norse explorers, sometimes called Vikings, probably were the first Europeans to reach Canada. A Norse group led by Leif Ericsson built a settlement on the tip of Newfoundland around A.D. 1000. The settlement was abandoned after about 30 years.

Other Europeans came to Canada about 500 years later. England employed Italian explorer John Cabot

◀ This painting shows Norse explorers sailing across the Atlantic Ocean. The Norse probably were the first Europeans to reach North America.

▼ Many European fur traders acquired furs from Aboriginal Peoples.

to find a new route to China. Cabot sailed west and reached Canada's coast in 1497. Cabot and his crew returned to England within a year. They reported that huge schools of fish near Canada slowed their ship. Soon, other people sailed across the Atlantic to fish off Canada's coast. Cabot's discovery led England to claim eastern Newfoundland.

The French also sent an expedition to the new land. In 1534, the French explorer Jacques Cartier landed on Prince Edward Island and the Gaspé Peninsula of Québec. He claimed this area for France. In 1535, Cartier traveled up the St. Lawrence River to Montreal.

The French began to settle Canada in 1604. A French expedition of 79 men spent the winter on the St. Croix River between New Brunswick and Maine. Samuel de Champlain was one of the 35 men who survived that hard winter. In 1605, he helped establish Port Royal in Nova Scotia with Pierre Du Gua de Monts. Port Royal became the first permanent European settlement in North America. In 1608, Samuel de Champlain founded the city of Québcc on the St. Lawrence River.

## French and English Rivalry

The French and English established more settlements during the 1600s. French villages and fur trading posts in Québec drew French settlers to the region. Many of these people were fur traders who trapped beavers, foxes, and bears. They also traded goods with Aboriginal Peoples for furs. The French sold the popular furs of these animals in Europe.

In 1670, England began to compete with France for control of the fur trade. King Charles II of

England chartered the Hudson's Bay Company. He gave the company the right to trap animals in a huge area of land surrounding Hudson Bay.

During the 1700s, Great Britain and France fought several battles for control of Canada. In 1759, Britain defeated France on the Plains of Abraham, an area just west of Québec City. After the fall of Québec City in 1759, Britain and France signed the Treaty of Paris in 1763. The treaty gave most of the French territory in eastern Canada to Great Britain. Great Britain gained control of the colonies of Québec, Nova Scotia, and Newfoundland, and regions that later became Ontario, New Brunswick, and Prince Edward Island. France kept two small islands near Newfoundland.

## Ethnic Tensions

Many French settlers in the colony of Québec worried about their future after Britain took control of Canada. In 1774, Britain passed the Quebec Act to calm the 65,000 French-speaking Canadians. The Quebec Act granted the people of French background the right to keep their French traditions, language, and culture while living in British-controlled land.

More settlers moved to the British colonies from the United States after colonists there defeated the British army in the Revolutionary War (1775–1783). These settlers, called Loyalists, wanted to remain loyal to

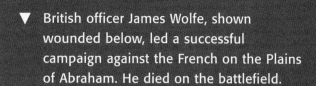

▼ British officer James Wolfe, shown wounded below, led a successful campaign against the French on the Plains of Abraham. He died on the battlefield.

Britain. They did not want to become citizens of the newly created United States. The increased number of English-speaking settlers in Canada created even more tension between the French and British Canadians.

In 1791, Britain tried to ease the cultural tensions in Canada by dividing the colony into two parts. Upper Canada covered the area near the Great Lakes and the upper St. Lawrence River. Canadians in

▼ During the War of 1812, U.S. troops attacked a fort on the border between New York and Canada during the Battle of Plattsburg.

Upper Canada followed British customs. Lower Canada occupied the area along the lower St. Lawrence River. Canadians in Lower Canada followed French cultural traditions. Britain allowed each region to have its own government.

Ethnic tensions were put aside when unsettled issues between the newly independent United States and Great Britain led to the War of 1812 (1812–1814).

Canada was the closest British colony to the United States. U.S. soldiers attacked Canada because of its ties to Britain. The war ended when British and U.S. leaders signed the Treaty of Ghent on December 24, 1814. Canada, Britain, and the United States have not fought against each other since the end of that war.

Following the war, fighting broke out in Upper and Lower Canada against the British government. The Canadian colonists felt that they were not well represented in the British-controlled government. Britain then joined Upper and Lower Canada into the United Province of Canada. In 1848, the province gained responsible government. The appointed officials became more accountable to the elected members of Canada's government. In this way, the government was more accountable to voters.

## Building a New Country

The colonies of Canada, Nova Scotia, New Brunswick, Prince Edward Island, and Newfoundland grew. But many people in the colonies thought that the United States had become too powerful after the American Civil War (1861–1865) ended. Canadians feared that the United States would try to take over their colonies. The colonists thought that they would be better able to protect themselves from the United States if the colonies united to become one country.

On July 1, 1867, the British North American Act united the colonies of Canada, Nova Scotia, and New Brunswick in a confederation called the Dominion of Canada. Ottawa had been selected the capital of the United Province of Canada in 1857. This city became the capital of the Dominion of Canada.

Other provinces joined the confederation. The provinces of Manitoba, British Columbia, and Prince Edward Island became part of the Dominion of Canada in the early 1870s. Saskatchewan and Alberta joined the confederation in 1905. In 1949, Newfoundland and Labrador became Canada's 10th province.

Two territories also became part of the early Dominion of Canada. In 1870, Britain gave control of the Northwest Territories to Canada. In 1898, the Yukon Territory was established.

The Dominion of Canada's military became a major participant in world military operations. It was active in World War I (1914–1918), World War II (1939–1945), and the Korean War (1950–1953). Canada joined the United Nations in 1945. Since then, Canada has been active in every major United Nations peacekeeping operation.

▼ Britain's Queen Elizabeth II signed the Constitution Act in April 1982.

Canada kept its strong ties with Britain. Canadians were British subjects until 1947. That year, Canadians were allowed to claim Canadian citizenship. Britain still held some power over Canada until 1982, when the British Parliament passed the Canada Act and the Constitution Act. These acts gave Canada the power to change its constitution. They also included a Charter of Rights and Freedoms.

▼ These Inuit live in the new Territory of Nunavut, which was created in 1999.

## Canada Today

Tension still exists between French-speaking and English-speaking Canadians. Some French-speaking Québec citizens want Québec to be independent from Canada. But in a 1995 vote, the majority of Québec voters decided to keep Québec as a Canadian province. The Canadian Parliament officially recognized Québec as a distinct society within Canada.

On April 1, 1999, Parliament created a new territory called the Territory of Nunavut. An Aboriginal Peoples group called the Inuit govern this territory. This land was carved from the eastern part of the Northwest Territories. Nunavut means "Our Land" in the Inuit language.

## Canada's Government

Canada has three levels of government. The federal government makes laws for the entire country. It deals with matters concerning the environment, relationships with foreign countries, and the defense of the nation. Provincial and territorial governments manage the needs of the people, such as education and health care. Municipal governments across the country manage towns and cities.

Canada's federal government is based on the British parliamentary system, which has three branches. Canada's executive branch includes the governor general and prime minister. Great Britain's king or

queen, on the advice of the prime minister, appoints a governor general as a representative and head of state of Canada. The governor general rarely has power in government. The actual leader of the Canadian government is the prime minister, who usually is the leader of the majority party in the House of Commons. The prime minister appoints a cabinet that usually is made up of members of the legislative branch, or Parliament. The prime minister and cabinet propose policies and laws to Parliament.

Parliament is divided between the Senate and the House of Commons. The Senate has 105 members. The governor general appoints senate members on the advice of the prime minister. Senators can serve until they are 75 years old. Canadian citizens hold elections to choose members of the House of Commons. Election dates are determined by the prime minister, but must be held at least every five years. The House of Commons has 301 seats. The Senate and the House of Commons pass bills. The governor general signs the bills into law.

Canada's judicial system follows the Canadian Constitution. The judicial branch includes courts established by provinces and by Parliament. The provincial court system has two levels. The first level is the Provincial Court, which mostly handles criminal cases. The second level includes the Superior Court and Court of Appeal. The Superior Court handles the most serious criminal and civil cases. The Court of Appeal hears cases from lower courts. Parliament created the Federal Court to handle patents, appeals, maritime law, and claims against the government. The highest court in the country is the Supreme Court of Canada. This court hears appeals from all lower courts and makes a final decision.

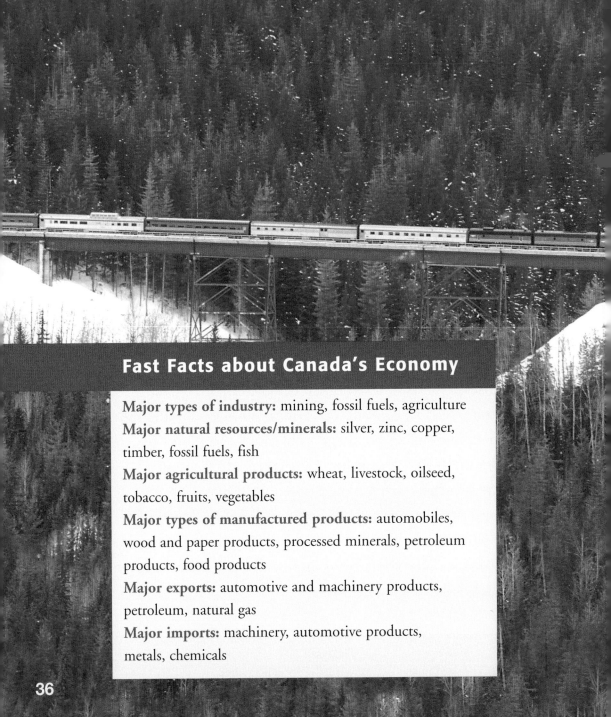

## Fast Facts about Canada's Economy

**Major types of industry:** mining, fossil fuels, agriculture

**Major natural resources/minerals:** silver, zinc, copper, timber, fossil fuels, fish

**Major agricultural products:** wheat, livestock, oilseed, tobacco, fruits, vegetables

**Major types of manufactured products:** automobiles, wood and paper products, processed minerals, petroleum products, food products

**Major exports:** automotive and machinery products, petroleum, natural gas

**Major imports:** machinery, automotive products, metals, chemicals

# Chapter 4

# Canada's Economy

Canada's economy is strong. The unemployment rate is low and the number of new jobs is growing. In most two-parent families, both adults work outside the home. Fewer than 20 percent of Canadian families are supported by one income. Women make up 45 percent of the Canadian workforce.

Transportation and communication systems are very important in a country of Canada's size. They help keep Canada's businesses running smoothly. Canadians have overcome difficult conditions such as permafrost to build railroads and highways in the northern regions. Canada also has a good air travel system that helps move goods and people quickly. The communication industry is one of Canada's largest service industries. Canadians develop effective ways to communicate over great distances using computers, telephones, and other technologies.

◀ Trains carry passengers and goods across Canada. The country's transportation systems are well maintained.

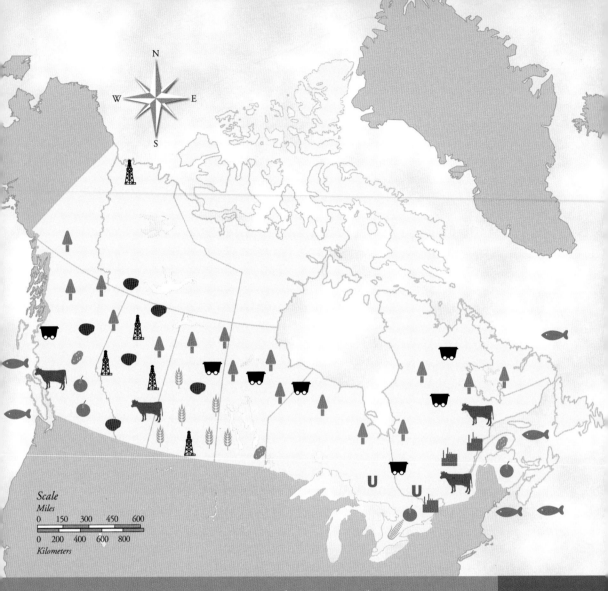

# Canada's Industries and Natural Resources

## KEY

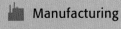 Coal  Manufacturing

Corn  Mining

 Fishing Oil

Forestry **U** Uranium

Fruit  Vegetables

Livestock Wheat/grains

## Agriculture and Fishing

Canada's wide-open spaces and rich soil make it one of the world's leading producers of agricultural products. Wheat is Canada's main crop. Farmers raise other grains, as well as tobacco, fruits, vegetables, and oilseeds. Most regions support livestock farms as well.

Varying climates and soil types split Canada into four major agricultural regions. Fruit and vegetable farmers in the Atlantic region grow apples, blueberries, and potatoes. Large food processing plants also are located in this region.

The Central region includes the provinces of Ontario and Québec. The rich lowland area near the St. Lawrence River is Canada's major corn-producing area. The mild climate of southern Ontario helps produce excellent harvests of grapes, cherries, peaches, and other fruits. The many sugar maple forests in this region allow farmers to collect large amounts of maple sap, which is used to produce maple syrup.

The plains of west-central Canada have some of the richest grain and oilseed fields in the world. About 80 percent of Canada's farmland is located in this region. Farmers there grow more than 50 million tons (45 million metric tons) of wheat, oats, barley, rye, canola, and flaxseed each year. Canola is used to make cooking oil and margarine. Flaxseed often is used in medicines. Livestock farmers in this region raise some of Canada's largest herds of hogs and cattle.

The area near the Pacific Ocean has many different climates and soils. Farmers grow grains and oilseeds in the northeastern part of the region. River valleys and grassland ranges support herds of beef cattle. The climate of the southern Cordillera is perfect for orchards and vineyards.

Fishing was one of Canada's first industries and it remains important today. Both the west and east coasts support large fishing industries. Fishers catch salmon on the west coast, while the east coast's waters provide cod, haddock, herring, mackerel, and shellfish.

## Energy, Natural Resources, and Manufacturing

Canada creates energy from a variety of sources. Crude oil found in western Canada is processed into petroleum and natural gas. Some of Canada's rivers have been dammed to produce hydroelectricity. Canada's many mines produce uranium and coal, which fuel power plants. Mines in the province of Alberta produce half the coal mined in Canada. Canada is the world's largest producer of uranium.

▼ Cattle and other livestock are a common sight on the plains of western Canada.

Miners dig for many other minerals in Canada. The country has large deposits of nickel, sulfur, silica, copper, and silver. Canada also is the world's largest producer of zinc and potash, which is used in fertilizer. Canada is the world's fifth leading producer of gold.

Forests cover almost 50 percent of Canada, making the country a leader in the forestry industry. Canadian forests provide the necessary resources for lumber, paper, and other wood products.

The sale of manufactured products brings more money into Canada than any other industry. Canada is active in the development of new technologies. Factory workers make computer products, motor vehicle parts, machinery, and telecommunications equipment.

## Service and Tourism

Manufactured products bring in the most money to Canada. But 75 percent of the workforce is employed in service jobs. Service workers have jobs in health services, education, and government. Trade, communications, and retail stores also employ service workers.

Tourism is one of Canada's largest service industries. Some tourism workers have jobs at

▼ This sawmill in Alberta processes trees into lumber.

▲ Festivals, such as this winter carnival,
draw visitors to Canada year-round.

Canada's 39 national parks and reserves and 849
national historic sites. People visit the West
Edmonton Mall in Edmonton, Alberta, which is the
world's largest mall. Canada's scenic landscape draws
campers, hikers, and other outdoor enthusiasts. A
variety of cultural events and festivals bring visitors
to Canada year-round.

## Canada's Money

The Canadian unit of currency is the dollar. One hundred cents equal one dollar. Exchange rates change every day. In the early 2000s, about 1.53 Canadian dollars equaled 1 U.S. dollar.

nickel

penny

$5 bill (back)

$20 bill

$1 coin

quarter

$2 coin

$5 bill (front)

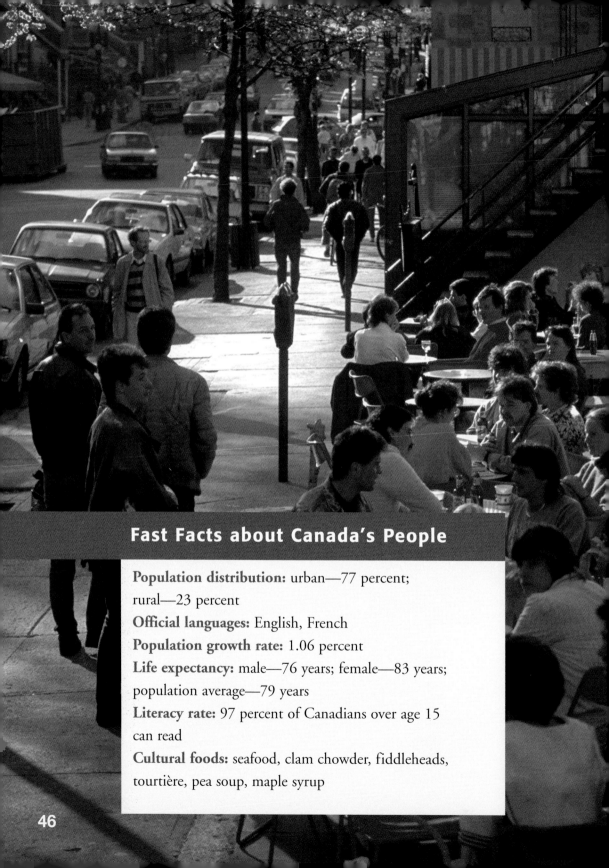

## Fast Facts about Canada's People

**Population distribution:** urban—77 percent;
rural—23 percent

**Official languages:** English, French

**Population growth rate:** 1.06 percent

**Life expectancy:** male—76 years; female—83 years;
population average—79 years

**Literacy rate:** 97 percent of Canadians over age 15
can read

**Cultural foods:** seafood, clam chowder, fiddleheads,
tourtière, pea soup, maple syrup

# Chapter 5

# People, Culture, and Daily Life

Canadians work hard to build a country where citizens of all backgrounds feel a sense of belonging. At one time, most Canadians claimed either a British or a French background. Canada now welcomes a steady flow of immigrants from around the world.

## Cultural Diversity

Immigrants from France and Britain were the first non-Aboriginal people to settle permanently in Canada. Today, 40 percent of Canadians have a British Isles background and 27 percent have a French background. Other European groups account for 20 percent of the population. Asians and Pacific Islanders make up about 6 percent of the population. Aboriginal Peoples make up 3 percent of Canada's population. About 2 percent of the population is African Canadian.

◄ Canadians work hard to build a country where citizens of all backgrounds feel a sense of belonging.

▼ More than three-fourths of Canadians live in cities and towns such as Québec (below).

Canada is a bilingual country. English and French are its two official languages. Many immigrants also speak languages that they brought from their homelands. One Canadian radio station broadcasts its programs in 30 languages. The original languages of the Aboriginal Peoples are called Aboriginal languages. The Aboriginal Peoples Television Network started in 1999 to provide news and entertainment for Aboriginal people in their own languages.

People who immigrate to Canada often keep their religious beliefs as well as their languages. Many French settlers were Roman Catholic. The majority of English settlers were Protestant. Today, 45 percent of Canadians are Roman Catholic, while 36 percent practice Protestant religions. The other 19 percent of the population practice a wide range of religious beliefs. The Mennonites, Doukhobors, Jews, and other religious groups came to Canada to practice their religions freely. Other immigrants brought Buddhism, Hinduism, Sikhism, and Islam. There is also a great deal of interest among Aboriginal Peoples in native spirituality.

## Living Conditions

In 1867, 10 percent of the Canadian population lived in cities and 90 percent lived in rural areas. Today, about 77 percent of Canadians live in cities and towns.

## Learn to Speak French

Canada has two official languages—English and French. Many Canadians are bilingual. They speak both languages. Canadian English is spelled like British English. Examples include colour (KUHL-ur), and centre (SEN-tur).

Some basic French words and pronunciations appear below.

**good-bye**—au revoir (oh ruh-VWAH)

**good morning**—bonjour (bohn-JOOR)

**thank you**—merci (mare-SEE)

**sorry**—désolé (day-zoh-LAY)

**please**—s'il vous plaît (SEEL VOO PLAY)

**no**—non (NOH)

**yes**—oui (WEE)

**Do you speak English?**—Parlez-vous anglais? (par-LAY-VOO on-GLAY?)

▲ Signs at the border and throughout Canada are in French and English, the country's two official languages.

Most Canadians have modern homes with many conveniences. Almost all Canadians have TV and phone service. Many people living in cities rent apartments. But the majority of Canadians own their own homes, most of which are designed for a single family.

## Education

Canada's high standard of education helps drive the quality of life in Canada. The country's literacy rate is 97 percent. Public education is free throughout the country. Each province runs its own schools. Children are required by provincial laws to attend school from age 6 or 7 until they are 15 or 16 years old. In some provinces, children enter kindergarten at age 4.

Children in rural areas often live far away from school. They travel long distances by bus for classes. Some children live in remote areas of Canada. These students may live at boarding schools or receive lessons from their teachers by using a computer.

Canadian students study a variety of subjects. Elementary classes focus on language, math, social studies, and science. Many children learn both English and French. High school students choose a path of study. One path prepares students to enter a university. The other path prepares students for community college, a school of technology, or the workplace.

▲ During winter, Canadians skate on frozen rivers. The Rideau Canal in Ontario is the world's longest skating rink.

## Canadian Arts and Pastimes

The arts have flourished in Canada since the Aboriginal Peoples arrived. Artists known as the Group of Seven are some of the most famous painters in Canadian history. Their paintings show the harshness of areas in the Canadian landscape. Canadians enjoy music of all types, including pop, Jamaican reggae, Celtic folk music, and jazz. Theater and dance are popular with many Canadians.

Many Canadians enjoy spending time outdoors. In Canada's wilderness areas, they camp, hike, fish, and hunt. During winter, Canadians ice skate on indoor rinks and frozen lakes and streams. They go cross-country and downhill skiing. Ice hockey, a sport invented in Canada, is a popular activity. Tennis, baseball, basketball, and golf are other popular sports that Canadians play. Lacrosse came from games played by Aboriginal Peoples. Both ice hockey and lacrosse are Canada's national sports.

## Traditional Foods and Holidays

Traditional Canadian dishes vary by region and culture. People in the Atlantic provinces and British Columbia often eat fresh seafood caught in their coastal waters. Clam chowder is a favorite in these regions. Fiddleheads are a favorite food in New Brunswick. People gather these tender fern shoots in forests in the spring. Cooks lightly boil these plants and serve them with butter. A tourtière is a traditional food served by French-Canadians in Québec. This meat pie is made with pork and served on Christmas Eve. Maple syrup is one food Canada claims as a national tradition. Canadians sometimes pour the syrup over pancakes, or on snow. They also eat it as a hardened candy.

Christian Canadians celebrate many holidays throughout the year. They celebrate Easter in early spring. Saint Jean-Baptiste Day, celebrated in Québec on June 24, began as a religious holiday honoring John the Baptist. Some Québec citizens observe this holiday by lighting bonfires. Christians throughout Canada celebrate Christmas on December 25.

All Canadians observe national holidays. Victoria Day on May 24 honors British Queen Victoria's birthday. On July 1, Canadians celebrate Canada's national founding on Canada Day. Labor Day on the first Monday in September is a tribute to all Canadian workers. In October, Canadians observe a national day of Thanksgiving. Remembrance Day on November 11 honors the men and women of Canada who fought for their country during wartime.

# Make Maple Ice Cream

Canadians use maple syrup to flavor a variety of dishes. They sometimes add maple syrup to snow or ice cream. Ask an adult to help you with this recipe for maple ice cream.

## What You Need

¾ cup (175 mL) heavy cream
3 tablespoons (45 mL) maple syrup
1 cup (250 mL) light cream
2 teaspoons (10 mL) vanilla extract
4 tablespoons (60 mL) powdered sugar
½ cup (125 mL) whole or 2% milk
additional syrup to pour on ice cream

measuring cups
measuring spoons
mixing bowl
whisk
potholder
medium saucepan
mixing spoon
medium container with lid

## What You Do

1) Whisk ¾ cup (175 mL) heavy cream and 3 tablespoons (45 mL) maple syrup in mixing bowl until stiff.

2) Gently heat 1 cup (250 mL) light cream, 2 teaspoons (10 mL) vanilla extract, 4 tablespoons (60 mL) powdered sugar and ½ cup (125 mL) milk in a medium saucepan. Cook over low heat, stirring continuously until sugar is dissolved.

3) Stir the heavy cream and maple syrup mixture into the saucepan ingredients. Pour into a medium container and cover with a lid.

4) Freeze mixture for about three hours or until firm.

5) Scoop ice cream into bowls and pour on additional maple syrup as desired.

Serves 4 to 6

▲ The Canadian National Tower in Toronto is the world's tallest free-standing structure. The tower is 1,755 feet (535 meters) tall.

# Canada's National Symbols

### ◄ Canada's Flag

Canada's national colors, red and white, are used in the flag. Red stands for England, while white represents France. The maple leaf in the center is Canada's national emblem. The flag, designed by Dr. George F. G. Stanley, was adopted in 1965.

### ◄ Canada's Coat of Arms

The shield on Canada's coat of arms has sections that represent England, Scotland, Ireland, and France. The maple leaves represent all of Canada's people. Canada's current coat of arms was drawn by Cathy Bursey-Sabourin in 1994.

## Other National Symbols

National tree emblem: maple tree

National animal emblem: beaver

National bird emblem: common loon

National anthem: "O Canada," music by Calixa Lavalleé, original French words by Sir Adolphe-Basile Routhier

National sports: ice hockey and lacrosse

# Timeline

**1608**
Samuel de Champlain establishes a permanent French settlement in Québec.

**1497**
John Cabot claims Canada's eastern coast for England.

**1759**
Britain defeats France on the Plains of Abraham.

| B.C. | A.D. | 1500 | 1600 | 1700 |
|------|------|------|------|------|

**9,000– 18,000 B.C.**
The first people arrive in North America.

**A.D. 1000**
Norse explorers build Canada's first European settlements.

**1534**
Jacques Cartier lands on Prince Edward Island and the Gaspé Peninsula and claims these areas for France.

**1610**
Henry Hudson explores Hudson Bay for England.

**1763**
The British and French sign the Treaty of Paris.

**1857**
Ottawa is chosen as the capital of the United Province of Canada.

**1947**
Canadians can declare citizenship for the first time.

**1982**
British Parliament passes the Canada Act, giving Canada full authority over its constitution.

**1800**

**1900**

**2000**

**1812–1814**
Canada fights as Britain's colony in the War of 1812 against the United States.

**1867**
British Parliament establishes the Dominion of Canada with the British North American Act.

**1965**
Canada adopts its official flag.

**1999**
Parliament establishes the Territory of Nunavut for the Inuit people.

# Words to Know

**fjord** (FYORD)—a long, narrow inlet of the ocean between high cliffs; fjords in Canada were formed by glaciers during the Ice Age.

**hoodoo** (HOO-doo)—an unusual rock formation shaped by wind and water

**hydroelectricity** (hye-droh-i-lek-TRISS-uh-tee)—electricity made from energy produced by running water

**Inuit** (IN-yoo-it)—a group of people who are descendants of the original people from the Arctic regions of Canada and Greenland; they once were called Eskimos; means "the people" in Inuit language

**permafrost** (PUR-muh-frawst)—subsoil in the Arctic region that remains permanently frozen

**rain forest** (RAYN FOR-ist)—a thick forest of tall trees and plants located in areas that are warm and rainy year-round

**telecommunications** (tel-uh-kuh-myoo-nuh-KAY-shuhns)—the science that deals with the sending of messages over long distances by telephone, satellite, radio, and other electronic means

**tundra** (TUHN-druh)—a frozen, treeless Arctic region

**uranium** (yu-RAY-nee-uhm)—a silver-white radioactive metal that is the main source of nuclear energy

# To Learn More

*The 1999 Canadian Encyclopedia: Student Edition.*
Toronto: McClelland & Stewart, 1999.

**Barlas, Robert, and Norman Tompsett.** *Canada.*
Countries of the World. Milwaukee: Gareth Stevens
Publishing, 1998.

**Grabowski, John F.** *Canada.* Modern Nations of the
World. San Diego: Lucent Books, 1998.

**Odynak, Emily.** *Early Canada.* Kanata, the Canadian
Studies Series. Calgary, Alberta: Weigl Educational
Publishers, 1998.

**Rogers, Barbara Radcliffe, and Stillman D. Rogers.**
*Canada.* Enchantment of the World. New York:
Children's Press, 2000.

# Useful Addresses

**The Canadian Embassy**

501 Pennsylvania Avenue NW

Washington, DC  20001

**National Library of Canada**

395 Wellington Street

Ottawa, Ontario  K1A 0N4

Canada

# Internet Sites

**Canada Information Office: Facts on Canada**

http://www.cio-bic.gc.ca/facts/index_e.html

Canadian government site covering a wide range of information

**The Canadian Encyclopedia Online**

http://www.thecanadianencyclopedia.com

A wealth of Canadian information compiled by 3,800 contributors

**CIA World Factbook—Canada**

http://www.cia.gov/cia/publications/factbook/geos/ca.html

Basic information from the U.S. Central Intelligence Agency

**Statistics Canada**

http://www.statcan.ca/start.html

Official data on population, land, and more

▲ The water crashing over Niagara Falls sends mist high into the air. Niagara Falls is located on the border of the United States and Canada.

# Index